THE ONE-ROOM SCHOOL
AT SQUABBLE HOLLOW

FIRST-GRADERS:

1. DANIEL LACROSS
2. KELLY LABREE
3. JASON GILMAN
4. HEATHER MCELROY

SECOND-GRADERS:

5. NATHAN STAHLER
6. NICOLE LACROSS
7. CASEY WILKERSON

THIRD-GRADERS:

8. LISA BICKFORD
9. CHRISTOPHER MCELROY
10. GRETCHEN HEIDT
11. AMY STEVENS
12. AMY JO BONA

FOURTH-GRADERS:

13. MELISSA DETH
14. CHRISTIE WILKERSON

FIFTH-GRADERS:

15. KRISTA DAY
16. ROBIN HAMEL

SIXTH-GRADERS:

17. DAN STAHLER
18. MATHEW GILMAN

TEACHER:

19. BARBARA BOSLEY

THE ONE-ROOM SCHOOL
AT SQUABBLE HOLLOW

ROSMARIE HAUSHERR

FOUR WINDS PRESS   NEW YORK

First Edition   Printed in the United States of America   10   9   8   7   6   5   4   3   2   1
The text of this book is set in 13 point Criterion Light.
The black-and-white photographs are reproduced in halftone.

Library of Congress Cataloging-in-Publication Data
Hausherr, Rosmarie. The one-room school at Squabble Hollow/Rosmarie Hausherr. — 1st ed.   p.   cm. Bibliography: p.   Summary: Text and pictures bring to life days at a one-room school in northern Vermont which has been functioning for more than 100 years.
  ISBN 0-02-743250-5
1. Squabble Hollow School (Caledonia County, Vt.) — Juvenile literature.   2. Rural schools — Vermont — Caledonia County — Juvenile literature. [1. Squabble Hollow School (Caledonia County, Vt.) 2. Schools.]   I. Title.   LD7501.C185H38   1988   370.19'346'0974334 — dc19   87-17774   CIP   AC

Writing and photographing the story of the Squabble Hollow one-room school has been a uniquely touching experience.

My warm thank-you goes to the children, parents, and people of Squabble Hollow; to Mrs. Bosley and all the other teachers for their support, patience, and enthusiasm; and to the Lyndonville School Board.

I am grateful to my editors: Meredith Charpentier, who initiated this project; Barbara Lucas, who guided me through it; and Cindy Kane, who gave it a happy ending. And special thanks to Lynne Arany for her creative book design.

A big thank-you to Raymond Marunas for being my writing coach, to William J. Lederer for his support and advice, and to the many friends and educators who helped.

Mrs. Jody Kenny from the Education Department, St. Michael's College, Winooski, Vermont, generously shared her research on one-room schools, as did Professor Leonard Johnson from the Castleton Teaching College, Vermont.

America's Country Schools by Andrew Gulliford (Washington, DC: Preservation Press, 1984) has been a valuable source of information on rural schools.

CONTENTS

~~~~

WELCOME TO SQUABBLE HOLLOW   1

PITCHING IN   4

FIRST DAY OF SCHOOL   8

CHORES TO CHIPS   17

READING, WRITING, 'RITHMETIC   23

A BUTTERFLY IS BORN   30

SONGS, SURPRISES, AND THANKS   36

ALLEN ARRIVES   44

EXERCISE AND CHICKEN SOUP   48

I CAN READ   53

SMILE, FLASH, CLICK!   56

ON THE AIR   59

MAKING AND WEARING THE MASKS   63

HALLOWEEN PARTY!   67

A NOTE TO EDUCATORS AND PARENTS
ABOUT ONE-ROOM SCHOOLS   74

WELCOME TO
SQUABBLE HOLLOW

Over a hundred years ago, the farmers who lived in the Squabble Hollow valley in northern Vermont built a schoolhouse for their children. It had only one room and one teacher. The children learned reading, writing, arithmetic, and religion from a blackboard and a few books. This small building had an outdoor bathroom, a wood stove, no electricity, and tiny windows; but the people of Squabble Hollow were proud to have a school.

The funny name, Squabble Hollow, went back to a squabble, or argument, the early settlers from the valley and the hill had over a kettle of corn pudding. A hollow is another name for a valley.

In 1929, after a fire, the Squabble Hollow people modernized their school. Larger windows and electric lights made learning easier. The students enjoyed more comfortable desks, their first indoor bathrooms, and their special pride—a piano! Only one thing remained the same: a single teacher taught all the grades, usually first through eighth. Over the years some 120 students have graduated from this public school. But it is more than a place where the children learn. The Squabble Hollow people meet at the school to make decisions or to celebrate their holiday parties together. The school is the heart of the community.

It has been a good summer for the children of Squabble Hollow. They fished and swam in the valley's shallow stream, sunned themselves on its smooth, warm rocks, and explored the riverbanks. Sometimes they went berry picking. Red raspberry juice stained their lips as they helped themselves to sweet berries, and the jars filled slowly. On rainy days they played in barns filled with sun-dried, sweet-smelling hay.

But the long vacation always ends, and now the children who have played together all summer long will learn together in their one-room school.

3

PITCHING IN

~

Bang, bang, bang!
"Hold it, Kenny!" a man's voice orders.
Bang, bang, bang!

"One, two, three . . . up!" a chorus chants. More hammering follows.

Every year before school starts, the Squabble Hollow parents, with love and pride, repair the old schoolhouse. They want the school to be as pleasant for their children as it was for them when they were students there. This summer they are replacing the old shed in back with a new room.

The children have come to watch the activities at the school. The younger children play while the older ones help their parents. They all enjoy eating sandwiches together and staying up late as the parents work into the night to finish their building on time.

"Lisa, dip just the tip of your brush into the paint," advises her mom. Lisa is slowly turning light blue, the color of the walls. The teacher, Barbara Bosley, in a paint-splattered T-shirt, works with the parents.

"I sure hope the paint will be dry by tomorrow," says Kelly's father to his neighbor.

"I'll let my electric fan blow overnight," replies Mr. Wilkerson, who is helping out with his tools.

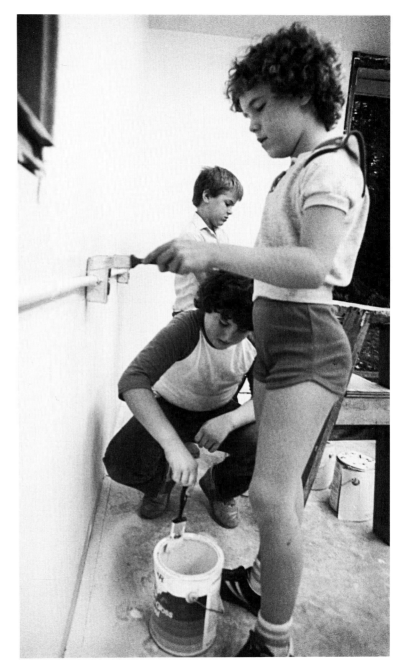

When the paint is dry and the bookshelves are finished, Mrs. Bosley begins stowing away the school supplies. Everything is covered with dust. The older children help to clean the books and games, the globe, the spider plant, the American flag. . . . As they touch the familiar objects they feel a growing excitement about returning to school.

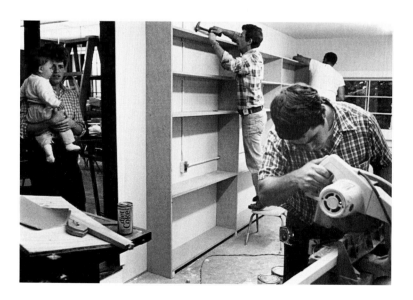

On Sunday, the last day of vacation, a team of men lay a blue, secondhand carpet from a local bank in the new room. Mathew's mother immediately begins to shampoo it. The old wooden classroom floor also gets a good scrubbing.

By late afternoon they are done. The school desks are lined up in straight rows. The classroom sparkles. Mrs. Bosley refills the chalk holder and tears the summer months off her calendar.

Everyone feels relieved and tired. With a last glance at their handiwork, they lock the door and go home for an early night's sleep.

FIRST DAY OF SCHOOL

~~~~

The yellow school bus stops, and the Squabble Hollow children hop off and walk the short stretch of dirt road to their schoolhouse. The girls are wearing their new outfits. They laugh at the boys running ahead.

Mrs. Bosley welcomes them all at the door.

"Oh, what a pretty dress, and I love the matching socks," she says to Kelly, who is a first-grader and a bit shy.

Lisa enters and gives Mrs. Bosley a big hug.

"You have a new haircut," her teacher says.

Lisa stretches a curl to her eyebrows. "Too short," she says. She takes Kelly, who is her cousin, to the coatroom.

A mother introduces her nine-year-old daughter. Mrs. Bosley says, "Welcome to the Squabble Hollow School, Melissa. I received your records, and I'm pleased to have such a fine new fourth-grader."

There are eighteen children in all, from first grade through sixth. The day starts with the Pledge of Allegiance. Then a fine dust rises from the piano keys as the teacher accompanies the children singing, "My Country 'Tis of Thee."

"Welcome back to school!" Mrs. Bosley says with a special welcome to the first-graders—Kelly, Heather, Jason, and Daniel. Then she introduces Melissa. "My name is Mrs. Bosley, but you may call me Mrs. B," she adds with a smile.

"I would like us to be a productive and happy school family. I expect the older students to help the younger ones and to set a fine example. Please be courteous."

"Mrs. B, when can we see the new room?" Nathan asks.

Mrs. Bosley smiles again. "First, I would like each of you to pick a desk and chair. Mathew and Dan, our senior students, will adjust the height for you."

After some commotion, the children end up in four groups with desks facing each other. "Mrs. B, can we see the back room now?" Gretchen asks impatiently.

"Ohh, it's beautiful!"

"I like the carpet!"

"It's big—big enough for a party."

"Yes, let's have a party."

"A party for our parents."

"What a nice idea!" Mrs. Bosley says.

Back in the classroom, they share happy memories from summer vacation.

"I won a blue ribbon showing my calf at the fair," Mathew says, his face beaming. Others tell of camping trips or visits to relatives in the city.

After the midmorning snack, the fifth-graders, Robin and Krista, hand out books, notebooks and folders, and a cup and toothbrush to every student. The children write their names in their new books.

Then, "Lunchtime!" Mrs. B says. The first lunchbox meal tastes great.

After recess, eighteen pairs of eyes focus on Mrs. B as she starts the afternoon by reading a story. The children love sitting on the carpeted floor in the new room. Now and then, the teacher asks an older student to explain a difficult word.

The afternoon ends with an art project, painting and cutting out paper apples.

"Can you hold my drawing?" Casey needs help from his sister, Christie. The children compare results and giggle.

At 2:30, Mrs. Bosley tells her students to clean their desks. Christopher helps Heather, his sister, with her backpack.

"Do you like school, Kelly?" Mrs. Bosley asks her new pupil. Kelly nods and smiles. From the school porch Mrs. B watches her students walk to the bus.

"I wonder what this school year will bring," Mrs. B says to herself when the children are gone.

She picks up a broom and thoughtfully sweeps the old, warped floor.

CHORES TO CHIPS

~~~~~

Good morning, children," Mrs. Bosley says in her usual cheerful manner. They look at her expectantly.

"First, let's talk about chores. Your parents worked hard to make our school beautiful. We want to keep it that way."

The children nod. "Mrs. Bosley, can I dust?" Gretchen asks.

Together, Mrs. B and the children make a list of eighteen chores and assign a person to each.

The children decide to rotate duties weekly: coatroom cleaning, taking out the garbage, kitchen duty, giving out the lunch milk, plant care. . . . Amy will collect the mail this week.

The least popular chore is toilet cleaning. Nathan is unhappy to be stuck with it first.

"Toilet-boy!" Jason teases.

Nathan turns around. "Shut up!" he says angrily.

After lunch the children play tag. Melissa still feels a little shy and watches from a distance. Then Heather trips and falls.

Dan helps her up. "My knee hurts!" Heather cries. Worse, she has lost one earring. Everybody searches in the grass.

"Here it is!" Melissa says. She puts the tiny silver star back in the girl's ear. Heather wipes her tears with her sleeve and smiles at Melissa. Hand in hand, they join the game.

A station wagon arrives and delivers a box. DOT MATRIX PRINTER, the carton says in bold letters.

"It's our computer printer!" the children say with pride. They earned the money for it, holding turkey raffles and a box-supper auction.

A gleaming piece of modern equipment emerges from between protective layers of packing material.

"Oooo, it's nice and shiny." Nicole touches it gently with one finger.

Connecting the printer to the computer turns out to be difficult.

"Children, please go to your seats and read," Mrs. B says. "I have to study the instructions."

After a few tries, the printer seems to work. The teacher allows the older students to run a test. "Wow!" they say as the machine zooms left and right, speedily printing the sentences they feed into the computer. The rest of the class gathers around, and each child takes a turn.

Later, the older students write letters with their computer printer to thank the local business people who gave building supplies for the new room.

READING, WRITING,
'RITHMETIC
~~~

The school days begin to fall into a pattern. Mrs. Bosley starts each day by explaining the schedule for the morning hours. Then she asks the first-graders to bring their phonics books to her table.

"Open to page eleven. Our new letter for today is *e*." The first-graders repeat *e* words after their teacher. "Egg, Eskimo, empty . . ."

Each grade takes its turn at her table while the other five study on their own. They know what subject to work on from Mrs. Bosley's weekly lesson plan. The older children are used to following written instructions.

The first-graders are getting restless. "What's the matter, Daniel?" Mrs. B asks.

"I don't know how to do this," he says.

"Amy Jo, would you please help him?" Mrs. Bosley asks an older student.

"Let's do a quick spelling test before recess," Mrs. Bosley says. Each student finds a partner. One reads, the other writes. They switch. Then they correct and grade each other's spelling. Christopher, who usually struggles with spelling, is proud today: not a single mistake!

"Ready for math?" Mrs. B asks her pupils after the break for recess.

"*Nnnooo,*" answers a chorus of voices.

She explains a math problem to the first-graders, who can't read instructions. While she teaches Christie and Melissa, her fourth-grade class, the noise in the classroom rises steadily.

"Quiet, please!" she says. For a short moment, only the shuffling of feet can be heard.

To Mathew, it seems that the hands of the old clock on the wall are standing still. For Lisa, who is struggling to finish her math before lunch, time is flying by.

"Keep going, Nicole." Dan encourages her. "Twelve plus thirteen equals how much?"

Nicole counts red and blue plastic chips. "Twenty-five?" she says. Dan nods. Nicole writes two crooked numbers.

"Sixth-graders, come up, please!"

Dan and Mathew are the next to join Mrs. B at her table.

"I believe you had problems on page forty-nine." Mrs. Bosley always remembers. They work on equations until the teacher finally says, "Lunchtime!"

"I made it!" Lisa shouts.

The afternoon starts with a song. Mrs. B at the piano misses the usual keys!

After story reading, all grades work on their English lessons. Toward the end of the afternoon Mrs. B says, "This has been a productive day, but you must learn to work more quietly. Now—let's square dance!"

"Yeahhhhhh!"

Mrs. Bosley puts a record on the old record player and calls the steps to the music. "Honor your partner!" Nathan bows to Heather. To the beat of the music the kids do-si-do, swing partners, promenade left, circle right. The younger children imitate the more experienced ones.

"Ouch!" screams Gretchen when Casey steps on her toes. Mrs. Bosley shows them a few new steps. They dance the Virginia Reel and then square dance until it's time to go home.

"Swing your partner . . ."

A BUTTERFLY IS BORN

The door bangs open the next morning, and Jason, sobbing loudly, walks straight to Mrs. Bosley's desk.

"He pushed me! Casey pushed me out of the sandpit."

"Did he?" Mrs. B says. "Why don't you wash your face, and then we'll talk about it."

When Jason returns from the kitchen, she asks, "What did you do before Casey pushed you?"

"Nothing," Jason says.

"Are you sure?"

"I only hid his truck," Jason admits.

"So, you made Casey angry." Jason nods. "I want you to return his truck and tell him you are sorry." He starts for the door. "Jason! We all love you," Mrs. Bosley adds.

Dense morning fog clings to the pine trees. Sleepiness hangs over the classroom. The children yawn from time to time. Suddenly Dan, who sits in the back of the room, jumps up and screams, "A butterfly is coming out!" All work stops, and everyone dashes to the science corner.

At the beginning of the school year, eight yellow, black, and white caterpillars came to live in a wire cage in the science corner, between the coatroom and the piano. The children have been feeding them milkweed leaves, which the caterpillars devour. One day, one of them fastened itself to the lid of the cage, head down.

By the next morning it had turned into a light green capsule, which in a few days turned black. "It's a chrysalis," explained Mrs. B. "The change from caterpillar to chrysalis to butterfly is called metamorphosis, a Greek word that means 'change of form.'"

Now the children, awestruck, watch the butterfly slowly unfold its crumpled wings.

"It looks like Mrs. Bosley's pocket umbrella," says Lisa.

"This is a monarch butterfly," Mrs. B says. "Who knows how he survives the winter?"

"He hides and sleeps?" says Christopher.

"Does he go to Florida?" asks Gretchen.

"No, your grandfather goes there," Mathew says with a grin. "The monarch migrates to Mexico."

"That's right," says Mrs. B. "It's a long trip for a butterfly, about five thousand miles."

"Five thousand. Wow!"

The children return to their seats, but they are too excited to concentrate on their English. They talk about how animals survive winter in the north: about migration, hibernation, and adaptation. Dan finds the definitions of these words in the encyclopedia.

Finally, the butterfly's wings are fully open. The children gather around their teacher, who lifts the butterfly out of the cage.

Outside, the sun has burned away the fog. The youngsters follow Mrs. B to the roadside. She sets the butterfly on a milkweed leaf.

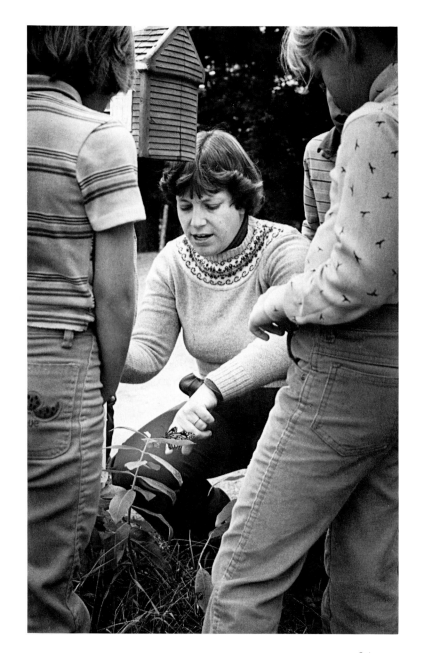

It seems to feel the sunlight on its beautiful black and orange wings. They flutter and the monarch lifts off, tumbling into the blue sky.

SONGS, SURPRISES, AND THANKS

~~~

The children are getting ready for Mrs. Miller's visit. With a guitar case in one hand and a tape recorder and bag in the other, she brings an hour of music to Squabble Hollow once a week.

The music teacher immediately begins to play the guitar and sing, "This land is your land . . ."

The children join in, but Mrs. Miller stops them. "Girls and boys, you can't sing like this." She tightens her mouth to look like the slit of a piggy bank. Everybody laughs. "Open your mouths wide! Aaaaaah! Let's try it again. 'This land is . . .,'" and the school fills with song.

After a few more songs, Mrs. Miller leans her guitar against a chair. "Today I'd like to tell you about the European composer Franz Joseph Haydn," she says. She plays a short piece of classical music on her tape player.

"I've heard this," several children say.

"It's from a TV cat-food commercial," says Amy.

"That's right," says Mrs. Miller. "But when Haydn wrote it in 1791, he called it the *Surprise Symphony*."

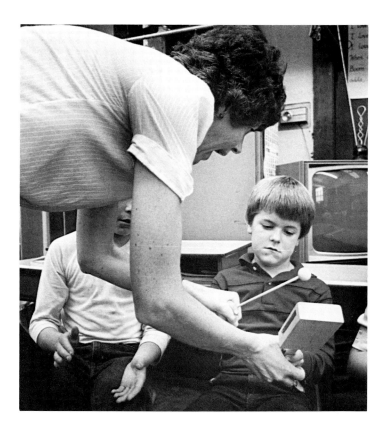

The music teacher hands out some woodblocks and sits down to play a new melody on the badly tuned piano. "Let's clap a steady beat to the next song," she says. Mrs. Bosley hums along while she covers the blackboard with a giant piece of paper.

Mrs. Miller checks her watch. "My goodness, if I don't run I'll be late for my class at the Red Village School! 'Bye, children. See you next week."

The parents' party is tonight. "Any ideas how to decorate our big poster for the party?" Mrs. B asks. "How about a big THANK YOU?"

After lunch, Mrs. Bosley outlines huge letters on the big paper with a large brush. The children fill them in with bright colors. Everyone pitches in, and the excitement begins to spread. They sweep the floor, wash the desk tops, and clean their guinea pig's cage.

Shortly after sunset, the guests arrive. Some carry foil-covered plates. The teacher's old table looks festive covered with a white cloth, flowers, and refreshments. Parents, neighbors, and the district principal admire the poster.

Everybody chats, jokes, and laughs.

Gretchen gives Melissa a guided tour of the cookie trays. "These brownies are my mom's; the ones with coconut are Grandma Gilman's; the raspberry squares are from Lisa's mom; and these . . . I don't know," she says, and grabs a handful.

Lisa and Kelly show off the new printer to their grandparents.

"My," Grandpa says, "you sure got some fancy machine here. When I went to Squabble Hollow School, we didn't have computers."

Lisa remembers a faded brown photograph showing a funny-looking boy, Grandpa, with his classmates and teacher outside the old school. She is proud that her grandfather went to this school, too—a long time ago.

43

ALLEN ARRIVES

~~~~~

At seven o'clock in the morning, Mrs. Bosley unlocks the door and carries two heavy bags of corrected work folders to her desk. She makes a cup of tea, greets Cinnamon, the guinea pig, and starts preparing for the new day.

At three in the afternoon she sweeps the schoolroom, checks the mail, and makes phone calls. She keeps track of money for book orders and the lunch-milk program, and prepares a field trip and a social studies project. Parents stop by to discuss their children. She writes school reports and sometimes attends school board meetings.

Mrs. Bosley is paid for her position as a teacher, but she is also a manager, janitor, nurse, and substitute mother.

"I fell in love with this school the moment I saw it," Mrs. B recalls. "That was five years ago, when Mrs. Farman, who had taught at Squabble Hollow for over thirty years, decided to retire."

But Mrs. Bosley could use some help!

Help arrives in a beat-up Chevy that stops outside the school with a loud bang. There is a short knock on the door, and a young man enters.

"Children, I want you to meet Allen Costello from Lyndon State College. Allen is our new student teacher. He will be with us two days a week," Mrs. Bosley says. She introduces each class to her new assistant.

"I'll bet he's a good ballplayer," Mathew specu-
lates out loud. Krista and Robin giggle. They think
Allen is cute!

The children take to their new student teacher in no time. They like his easy ways and ready smile, which shows a chipped tooth.

Allen helps Mrs. Bosley with teaching and helps the students with their work. He finds out how Mrs. Bosley makes her lessons interesting and how she prepares her teaching schedule.

Allen's chance to be a teacher at a one-room school is slim. There are only six left in Vermont.

During recess, Allen *is* a great ballplayer—a boost to any team. The children love to lean against his avocado-colored Chevy and bombard him with questions: "Do you play guitar?" "Did you chip your tooth playing volleyball?" "Do you have a girlfriend?"

Allen laughs. "Hey, guys, that's enough. Am I being interviewed?"

47

EXERCISE
AND CHICKEN SOUP

~~~

Christie, would you and Melissa like to correct the first- and second-grade work folders?" Mrs. Bosley asks the two girls as they enter. Christie and Melissa use Mrs. B's teacher's manual, and their manners are just like hers.

"Jason, would you please come here?" Christie calls in a grown-up voice.

"What is it?" he asks, eager to go out and play.

Christie points to the open folder. "Your math page is not finished," she says. Jason grabs the page and sits down. "Print the numbers neatly," Christie says.

"Okay, teach!"

By midmorning, the gym teacher, Judy Sherburne, arrives. She teaches physical education to all the elementary school classes in the Lyndon School District.

Squabble Hollow doesn't have a gym. In bad weather the students move their desks and exercise in the classroom. Mrs. Sherburne teaches special indoor games.

Today the sun is shining. At the sound of Mrs. Sherburne's whistle, everyone gets in line for warm-up exercises outdoors.

"One, two, one, two . . ." Mrs. Sherburne moves vigorously. Across the road, the cows stop grazing and stare for a while.

The children hold Mrs. Sherburne's colorful nylon parachute.

"Swing your arms high," she says. "One, two, three!" A pretty orange and yellow dome inflates above their heads. The children raise dome after dome. They are strengthening their muscles, but only Mrs. Sherburne knows that!

"Let's sit and hide our legs under the parachute," the gym teacher says. "Now we'll pretend that Dan is a hungry shark. Dan," Mrs. Sherburne says, "crawl underneath and pull someone's leg." The children scream. Now Amy Jo is the shark.

"Watch out for my smelly socks," Christopher says, grinning.

The next game, Charlie over the Water, is the younger children's favorite. Too soon, it's time to go back to the classroom.

Mrs. Bosley asks her students to open their math books.

"Not math again," Krista says. She angrily writes in her notebook for a while. Suddenly she rips out the page and shouts, "I'll never learn these fractions! Never!" and buries her head in her arms.

Mrs. Bosley calmly rises. "I'm going to cook chicken soup for lunch while you all finish math."

"Yeah, chicken soup!" the children cheer.

"Krista, bring your math book and come with me to the kitchen," Mrs. Bosley says. While stirring the soup, she patiently explains fractions until Krista smiles and says, "I think I got it." Mrs. Bosley gives her a hug and announces lunch.

I CAN READ

K elly likes to arrive early, before everybody else. This morning, she opens her bag and looks at a picture book. The humming of the overhead lights, the turning of pages, and the gurgling from the aquarium are soothing sounds.

An explosion of shouts and footsteps ends the peaceful quiet. The school day begins.

"Casey, you read first today," says Mrs. Bosley. Casey prefers math to reading. He likes playing with his minitrucks even better. He hides a few of them inside his desk. When it's safe, he runs one of them up and down his leg.

Casey needs extra help with reading. He reads aloud in a flat voice, cautiously, as if the words might break. Mrs. Bosley is patient with Casey, hoping one day the words will come alive for him.

Kelly suddenly grabs her friend's arm. "Heather! I can read this book," she whispers excitedly. "Listen!" She reads in a low voice, "On a chair . . ."

From her table, Mrs. Bosley observes the two girls. "Children," she says to the class, "Kelly has something wonderful to share with you."

Surprised by the sudden attention, Kelly stands up and says shyly, "I can read."

At the end of the school day, Kelly's mother stops by with Erin, Kelly's younger sister. "Mom, I'll tell you a secret," Kelly says. "I can read!"

SMILE, FLASH, CLICK!

~~~

O h, no! We forgot to wear our nice shirts," Dan says to his younger brother Nathan when they arrive in the morning and see Mrs. B in her pretty outfit. They phone home and ask their mom if she will bring their favorite shirts.

The school photographer arrives after lunch. Allen gives her a hand unloading her equipment.

"I have a present for you." The photographer gives a comb to each child. Immediately the children have fun improving each other's hairstyles. With a moist handkerchief, Mrs. B checks faces for lunch leftovers. Nathan and Dan change into checked shirts.

"Who is first?" the photographer asks.

Nobody moves. The girls giggle, and the boys push each other.

"I'll be first," says Mrs. Bosley. She sits in front of the painted backdrop and faces the camera.

Her students chant, "Cheeeeeeeeeeeeeeese!"

"Smile!" *Flash! Click!*

Now the children take turns.

"Smile!" *Flash! Click!*

"How does the light know when to flash?" Christopher wants to know after everyone's picture has been taken. The photographer explains how her equipment works and permits the children to look into the camera.

"Your pictures will be mailed in three weeks. I hope you'll like them," she says on her way out.

ON THE AIR

A chilly fog hides the schoolhouse in layers of milky cotton when the children exit from the bus this morning. They are bundled up in quilted jackets, knitted hats, and gloves. A small group of girls are talking intensely, their breath turning into mist.

"My mom bought brown material for my bear costume," Gretchen says.

"I won't tell you what I'm going to be at the Halloween party," Lisa says, then turns to her cousin and whispers softly.

"What?" Kelly says, her ears hidden under rabbit-fur muffs.

Lisa whispers again, "A . . ."

"A witch!" Amy Jo says triumphantly. Lisa, annoyed, runs into the schoolhouse.

There is never enough elbow room in the tiny coatroom. Christopher frantically searches his bag. He can't find his newspaper, the *Weekly Reader*. He needs to report on it this morning. "I'm going to be in trouble," he sighs.

"This is WSQUAB, your local Squabble Hollow radio station. I'm Robin Hamel, this week's newscaster. Our first report today comes from"—Robin looks over the class—"Daniel!"

Daniel, a first-grader, tells his story from cartoons.

"Louder!" his audience requests.

"It's about a baby elephant," he repeats.

Mrs. Bosley sits on a small stool at the back of the room. Christie's news story is about hunger in Africa. She has memorized most of the information from the *Weekly Reader*. Her audience listens with interest.

Mathew, with a self-assured manner, takes his time adjusting the mike. The class loves a good performer. Mathew doesn't disappoint them with his lively report on NASA. Mrs. Bosley applauds.

"Hey, Casey, your face is dirty," says Gretchen when Casey gets up to speak.

"You can't see it on the radio," he answers. He starts telling a funny joke but can't stop laughing. Before he gets to the punch line, he has the entire class roaring.

The principal, on a routine visit, has entered and is standing next to Mrs. Bosley.

"This radio program sure teaches the students to speak to an audience," he says.

"Yes, and I can tell who has read the newspaper and who hasn't!" Mrs. B replies.

MAKING AND WEARING
THE MASKS

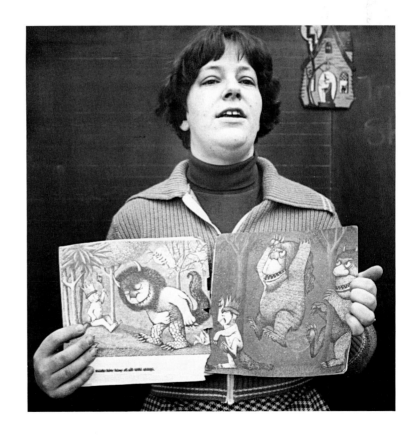

A ttention, attention! We're skipping story reading today because we have a busy afternoon. We are going to make our masks for tomorrow's Halloween parade in Lyndonville," Mrs. Bosley announces after lunch. "Please find the box you brought."

A week ago, the class had chosen their Halloween parade theme: Wild Beasts, inspired by Maurice Sendak's book *Where the Wild Things Are*.

The children go into action. Mrs. Bosley hands out jars of paint. Allen makes sure each child has a brush.

On the newspaper-covered desks, the brown cardboard boxes turn into brightly colored cubes.

While the painted boxes dry, Mrs. Bosley demonstrates how to shape eyes, ears, and noses.

"Use your imagination. Go wild!" she says.

"My ears won't stick," Heather says.

Amy Jo slides her mask over her head. "You look just like Mrs. B," Dan teases.

Casey will be king of the Wild Beasts. From large cardboard pieces, Allen cuts a boat for him. Casey paints it fiery red and writes MAX on the port side. While Mrs. Bosley makes a gold crown, Allen attaches straps to the boat so that Casey can carry it.

The children try on each other's masks, and the classroom fills with laughter. Mrs. B announces, "It's time to wash desks and stow away supplies. If we finish quickly, we'll put on our masks and go for a short walk before meeting the bus."

On a quiet country lane, a band of children turns into a horde of snarling, growling animals.

HALLOWEEN PARTY!

~~~~~~

The sky is deep blue and the air crisp on Halloween day. The sun casts long shadows by early afternoon.

Max and his Wild Beasts arrive in Lyndonville, where they meet children from other elementary schools. To the brassy sound of the high school band they walk slowly, hidden behind their masks, past parents and townfolk. "Grrrrrr, nghhhhhhhhhhh, jauhhhhhhhhhh . . ." The Wild Beasts from Squabble Hollow are a scary bunch!

They pose for a class picture, and each child is glad to get a lollipop: the snarling and growling has dried out their throats.

Back at the school, the children decorate the classroom for tonight's Halloween party.

Early nightfall glides silently through the black pines over the schoolhouse. In the cozy, well-lit homes along the valley, people are busy preparing for the Halloween party. It's the biggest event of the school year.

The first set of headlights illuminates the entrance of the school. The guests file into the warm room.

Here they come! Witches and princesses, cowboys and vagabonds, cooks and beggars. There is much surprise and laughter when Mrs. B arrives as . . . Mrs. Bee!

The children in their colorful outfits are eager to line up for the costume competition. Each one hopes to win a prize for the prettiest, the scariest, the funniest, or the most original costume.

The large table is stacked high with nicely decorated boxes. They each contain a dinner for two and are sold to male bidders only. The buyer will share his box dinner with the girl or woman who prepared it.

"Five dollars, five-fifty, six dollars, six-fifty . . ." Mathew's father, a skilled auctioneer, glances around the crowded schoolroom. "Six-fifty! Sold!" The crowd cheers.

From the sales, a happy Mrs. Bee receives $278.75 for the school's savings account. With this money they can make special purchases or go on field trips without financial help from the school board. The parents take pride in this independence.

After dinner, the older students receive visitors in their haunted house. "Ehhhhhhh! Uhhhhh!" The little children clutch their parents' sleeves.

The evening ends with apple dunking. Mrs. Bee is the first who has to dip her head into the water. Children and parents are having a wonderful time together.

But slowly the eyelids of the little ones begin to grow heavy.

"Good-night!" "Happy Halloween!" "See you tomorrow!"

Cheerful wishes float over the schoolhouse through the pine trees toward a cool moon. In the empty classroom, a happy mouse nibbles her free box dinner.

72

Mrs. Bosley and the children continue learning together, sharing their failures and successes, for the rest of the school year, until the summer vacation begins.

A NOTE TO EDUCATORS AND PARENTS
ABOUT ONE-ROOM SCHOOLS

One-room schools date back over 250 years in this country. The schools built by early settlers were usually primitive structures, chilled by drafts, heated by smoky wood stoves, poorly illuminated, with long splitwood benches to sit on and outhouses for toilets.

In a typical school, one teacher instructed pupils ranging from age four to age eighteen. The children often walked long distances to school, sometimes barefoot. During the busy farm seasons, older children left school to work at home. A well-worn blackboard, a few books, maps, and a Bible were often a teacher's only school supplies. Many teachers were themselves minimally educated. They earned low wages and usually boarded with local families.

Throughout the nineteenth century the quality of rural education varied according to the financial resources and the interest of a community. Eventually certification of teachers and the demand for more books and better-maintained school buildings improved the standards of some of the one-room schools. In many rural settlements those schools also functioned as the community center.

Today's one-room schools like Squabble Hollow still have a quaint rural look, but their cheerful classrooms contain modern conveniences and up-to-date school supplies, even microcomputers. What has not changed is the community's involvement and support and the importance of the teacher. These make a positive learning environment possible—academically, emotionally, and socially.

Small classes in one-room schools promote intensive student-teacher interaction and intimacy. The teacher focuses on the pupil's individual educational needs: gifted students advance into higher-grade activities and slow learners progress at their own pace, often with the aid of visiting special-education teachers. In a one-room school, helping each other is encouraged, which develops community spirit and a strong sense of belonging. The students are enriched for the rest of their lives.

One-room schools have been disappearing in this country since the beginning of the twentieth century. The 1920 U.S. Census listed 187,948 one-room schools. By 1947, the number had dropped to around 75,000; and by 1984, there were only 835 in just twenty-eight states. The push to consolidate, centralize, and standardize schools; better transportation; growth in suburbs, cities, and industrial areas—all have contributed to their demise.

In the state of Vermont, one-room schools are almost extinct. They dwindled from 1,571 schools in 1900 to 6 in 1985. Soon there may be none. At the end of the 1986 school year, the Lyndonville District School Board discontinued Squabble Hollow as a multigrade, one-teacher school. The children were bused to different schools in the area. Mrs. Bosley took a position as a prekindergarten teacher. The change deeply disappointed the children, their parents, and the community.

In modern education, open classrooms, multi-age grouping, peer teaching, and other experimental concepts are generally adaptations of teaching techniques successfully applied for years in one-room schools. It is up to educators, parents, and communities to preserve the one-room school's unique learning environment and to bring its spirit and traditional values into contemporary education.